Elves Don't
Wear Hard Hats

There are more books about the Bailey School Kids!
Have you read these adventures?

Elves Don't Wear Hard Hats

by **Debbie Dadey**
and
Marcia Thornton Jones

illustrated by **John Steven Gurney**

A
LITTLE APPLE
PAPERBACK

SCHOLASTIC INC.
New York   Toronto   London   Auckland   Sydney

For our number one Fan!
— M.T.J. and D.D.

ISBN 0-590-22637-1

12 11 10 9 8 7 6 5 4 3 2   6 7 8 9/9 0/0

Printed in the U.S.A.   40

First Scholastic printing, November 1995

Book design by Laurie Williams

Contents

1

New Playground

"It's my turn," Eddie yelled. "You've been swinging for an hour."

"I have not," Melody stopped her swing and jumped off. "Recess just started two minutes ago."

Their friends Liza and Howie stood between them. "Don't get all upset," Liza said. "We have to take turns."

Howie nodded. "Two swings are not enough for the whole third grade."

"We need new swings," Eddie complained. "These are so old, they came over on the *Mayflower*."

"This thing should be taken to the dump," Howie agreed and kicked the swing with his foot.

"It will be," Liza told them. "My mother

1

told me the PTA finally approved the money for fixing up the playground. We're going to have new equipment and everything!"

"Your mom would know," Eddie laughed. "Carey said your mom was trying to take over the playground committee."

"She was not," Liza sputtered.

Melody clapped her mittens together to make her friends stop fighting. "Who cares what Carey thinks as long as we're getting a new playground. When will they start?"

Liza didn't get a chance to answer because five huge green trucks rolled onto the snowy playground. One of the trucks pulled a small trailer. The signs on the side of each truck read: *Bell Construction Company*. As the kids watched, men jumped out of each truck, their tool belts jingling. The men weren't huge like the trucks, they were very short.

"I bet they're the ones who are going to put up our new playground," Liza said.

"Come on," Melody said. "Let's ask."

Melody ran up to a man climbing down from the first truck. He wore a bright green construction hat and work boots so old and worn, the toes curled up. Hammers, screwdrivers, and pliers of every sort hung from the tool belt around his waist. He was just a little taller than Melody.

"Hi!" Melody said. "Are you going to build our new playground?"

"Greetings," the little man said. His voice was high and squeaky. "My name is Hollis Bell and we're going to build you the best playground you can imagine!"

"All right!" Eddie cheered.

"Can we watch?" Liza asked.

"Sure," the man said. "Just stay clear

of the big trucks." Hollis Bell paused for a minute, looked at Eddie, and then pointed to the trailer behind one of the trucks. "But whatever you do, don't go near that trailer!"

2

Oh, Christmas Tree

"I can't believe how different it looks," Liza said. Melody, Howie, and Eddie nodded. The old swing set was gone and the playground looked bare. It was the next morning before school and the four friends stood under the giant oak tree in the school yard. Mr. Bell and the rest of his crew were busy cleaning up the playground. They whistled Christmas songs and their tool belts jingled every time they moved.

A few parents had gathered nearby to watch, too. "This new playground will cost a fortune," Carey's father complained.

"I still think the old equipment was fine," the lady wearing a scarf over curlers snapped.

"You've lost your gumdrops," a tall man with curly blond hair said. "That playground wasn't safe anymore!"

Then all the parents started talking at once. Melody sighed. "Parents never agree on anything."

"Well, I agree that the old playground needs help," Howie said with a nod. "Good-bye to that old swing."

Liza smiled. "We had a lot of good times on it, though."

"But think of the good times we'll have on the new equipment," Melody told her.

Eddie stood and watched the small men. He didn't say anything as they put the old playground equipment into a pile and then went inside the trailer.

"Why are you so quiet?" Howie asked him.

"I was just wondering," Eddie told him, "how can we find out what's in that trailer?"

"You can't," Liza told him. "Mr. Bell told us to stay out."

"Exactly," Eddie said. "And why would he say that?"

"Because he doesn't want you to see what's inside," Melody said.

"Right again," Eddie told her. "Don't you think that's odd?"

Liza shook her head so hard her hat fell off. "Mr. Bell probably heard about you and he doesn't want you messing with his stuff."

"Maybe," Eddie said slowly. "Or else he's hiding something from us."

"Yeah," Howie giggled. "Like the screw we need to replace the loose screw in your head!"

"Very funny," Eddie said. "But I plan on taking a look in that trailer!" Eddie stomped off, leaving footprints in the snow.

Melody, Liza, and Howie followed their

friend to the trailer sitting at the far end of the playground. Pounding noises and laughter could be heard coming from inside.

"What are they doing in there?" Eddie whispered.

Howie shrugged. "They're probably taking a coffee break."

"Sounds more like they're building something," Liza said.

Eddie hopped up and tried to peek in a window, but Christmas wrapping paper covered the glass. "Let's try a window on the other side," Eddie suggested as he started around the trailer.

"Wow! Look at that!" Eddie gasped.

The four friends stared at a row of twelve evergreen trees. Tiny candy canes dangled from the branches, and bright lights twinkled merrily.

"Ha, ha, ha! He, he, he! I'm glad you like my Christmas trees!"

The four friends jumped at the happy voice from behind them. There stood Hollis Bell. When he walked up to the kids, the tools hanging from his belt knocked together with a loud jingle.

"I just couldn't do without a little holiday cheer," he told Eddie. "And those trees remind me of home!"

"You're right about one thing," Eddie muttered. "There isn't much holiday cheer around Bailey City."

"Everyone's too busy fighting about our playground," Liza agreed.

"Each one of you has special magic to fix that sort of problem," Mr. Bell said with a wink. With that he hopped up the four steps to the trailer door and disappeared inside.

"That's strange," Eddie said.

"Lots of people like trees," Liza said.

"That's not what I'm talking about," Eddie snapped. "I meant that it's strange how Mr. Bell sneaked up on us."

Howie shrugged. "We were so busy looking at those trees, we just didn't hear him."

"How could we not hear those tools?" Eddie asked.

"Eddie's right," Melody interrupted. "Whenever Mr. Bell moves, those tools sound like Santa's jingle bells."

"And what about the trees?" Eddie hissed. "They weren't there before."

13

"Where did they come from?" Liza squeaked. "Christmas trees just don't spring up overnight!"

"Exactly!" Eddie sputtered. "There's something weird going on around here, and I think Mr. Hollis Bell has something to do with it. And I'm going to find out!"

3

Making a List,
Checking It Twice

That same afternoon their teacher, Mrs. Jeepers, stood at the front of the room and waited for the third-graders' attention. Everybody sat up straight and listened. Mrs. Jeepers had a way of getting their attention by flashing her green eyes and rubbing the mysterious brooch at her throat. Some of the third-graders even thought she was a vampire.

"We have a very special guest who would like to discuss something important with you," Mrs. Jeepers said in her strange accent.

Eddie waved his hand high in the air and waited for Mrs. Jeepers to call on him. "Are we in trouble?" he asked.

Mrs. Jeepers smiled an odd little half-smile and shook her head. "Quite the opposite. Mr. Hollis Bell would like to hear your ideas for the new playground." Then Mrs. Jeepers opened the classroom door.

Hollis Bell took off his green hard hat and bowed to Mrs. Jeepers. Hollis Bell made Mrs. Jeepers look like a giant. He only came up to the belt on her polka-dotted dress. When he walked into the room, the tools on his belt clanged together.

"Good afternoon, Bailey third-graders," he said. "The other helpers and I need your suggestions. What would you like for your playground?"

"You mean we get to plan it?" Howie asked.

"He, he, he! Ha, ha, ha!" Hollis Bell laughed. "What better way to plan the perfect place for such good boys and girls. Remember, magic happens when we work together!"

Liza raised her hand. "I'd like a brand-new set of swings."

"I want picnic tables," a fat boy named Huey called out.

"What about slides?" asked Melody.

"And a tree house!" Eddie hollered.

Carey waved her hand in the air. "All that's too expensive," she said in a squeaky voice. "My dad has it all planned out what we should do. He should know because he's the president of Bailey City Bank."

"Your dad can't do that!" Huey yelled. "My mother said so, and she's the PTA president. So there!"

"My, my, my!" Hollis Bell interrupted. "People seem to have many different ideas about this playground. So the other helpers and I want you to make a list. Write it carefully, and check it twice. Then we can get started on building the perfect playground."

"Are you going to use all our ideas?" Howie asked.

"He can't," Carey told the class.

Hollis Bell acted like he didn't hear her. "It is our job to make wishes come true. Put down your ideas, and we'll see what we can do!"

"But what if someone puts down a bad idea?" Liza asked.

"Ha, ha, ha! I'll know if it is good or bad, so make it good for goodness' sake!" And then Hollis Bell skipped out of the room with his tool belt jingling.

"Whoever heard of kids making a wish list!" Eddie laughed.

"I have," Liza said seriously. "I make a list every Christmas."

"That's different," Howie told her. "Lots of kids make a list for Santa Claus. But Hollis Bell is no Santa Claus, he's too short."

Melody giggled. "He's more the size of an elf!"

Eddie's eyes got big and he snapped his fingers. "That's it! I just figured out what's so strange about Hollis Bell."

4

Naughty or Nice

Eddie waited until recess to tell his friends about Mr. Bell. When they were under the oak tree he looked at each of his friends and spoke seriously. "Something is very different about Hollis Bell," he said.

Liza pulled her wool hat over her blonde hair and looked at Eddie. "Don't go making fun of him just because he's short. He can't help that."

"He's so short if he pulled up his socks, he couldn't see," Eddie said. "But that's not what I'm talking about."

Melody rolled her eyes. "Then exactly what are you talking about?"

"I'm talking about elves," Eddie said.

Melody looked at Howie. Howie looked

at Liza. They all looked at Eddie and started laughing. "Elves?" Melody said, holding back a giggle.

Eddie's face turned red. "It's not funny. I think Mr. Bell and his men are a bunch of elves."

"You mean like in Santa and his elves?" Liza asked.

Eddie shrugged. "I'm not sure about Santa, but I'm certain these guys are elves."

"If they're elves, then where's Rudolph and the other reindeer?" Howie asked with a smile on his face.

"You can joke all you want," Eddie said. "But you can't tell me it's normal for so many trees to get planted that quickly." He pointed to the playground. At least fifty brand-new evergreen trees went around the outside of the playground. All the trees were decorated with lights and candy canes. A few kids were

already picking the candy canes off the trees and eating them.

Liza gasped. "Where did those come from?"

"Elves," Eddie said.

Howie shook his head. "There has to be some other explanation."

"Nobody can plant that many trees that quickly without some kind of magic, let alone decorate them," Eddie said.

"It always takes my dad at least a week just to untangle the Christmas tree lights," Liza said.

"I think you two have had too much Christmas candy," Melody said. "Mr. Bell is short, but he's not an elf."

"Mr. Bell did say that all those Christmas trees reminded him of home," Liza told them. "Maybe he is from the North Pole!"

"I doubt if elves plant trees," Howie told them. "And I'm pretty sure they don't wear hard hats."

"There's one way to find out for sure," Liza said softly.

Eddie smiled as if he read her mind. "And that's exactly what we're going to do."

"You're not talking about messing around that trailer again," Melody warned. "Mr. Bell told us to stay away from it!"

"I'm not going to mess around it," Eddie told her.

"Good," Melody interrupted.

"I'm going to go in it," Eddie said.

"What?" Melody, Liza, and Howie said together.

Eddie pointed to the trailer. "Something is going on in there, maybe something bad."

"Something bad is what you'd be doing if you go in there," Melody reminded him.

Eddie shrugged. "It will be worth it to protect the school."

"Protect the school from what?" Howie asked. "A bunch of elves?"

"Elves are nice," Liza whispered.

Eddie looked to see if Mrs. Jeepers was watching. She was standing across the playground with her back turned to them. She seemed busy talking to a group of girls. "We can't be sure they're nice," Eddie said, "and I don't want to take any chances."

Without saying anything else, Eddie walked quickly toward the trailer. He stopped when he was on the far side. Right behind him were Melody, Howie, and Liza.

"I thought you didn't want to do this," Eddie whispered.

Melody looked at him. "We just came along to keep you out of trouble."

"We're not going in," Howie said. "We'll just peek in the door."

Eddie smiled and looked around the

playground. The men from Bell Construction Company were hard at work, digging more holes for trees. Mrs. Jeepers still had her back turned to them. Eddie took a deep breath and crept up the stairs to the trailer.

Slowly, Eddie pushed the door open. The four kids peered inside and gasped.

"Holy Toledo!" Eddie said. "They really are elves!"

His three friends didn't say anything.

They were too busy looking inside the trailer. Tables were squeezed into every available space and each table was covered with toys. There were dolls in doll beds, baseballs in gloves, bicycles that were partly put together, and even a huge dollhouse that took up an entire table.

"Wow!" Liza squealed. "It looks like a toyland in here."

"An elf toyland," Eddie reminded her.

5

Good Little Boy

"I told you," Eddie said after school. "They're elves!"

"You don't know that," Melody told him. She sat down under the oak tree and looked at Eddie.

"If they are not elves then why do they have a toy workshop in their trailer?" Eddie asked.

Howie held up his hand. "They probably have a good reason. We still don't have any proof that they're elves."

Eddie pointed at the playground. A huge area had been plowed, covered with pea gravel, and surrounded by a heavy wood border. "I do know," Eddie said, "nobody works that fast unless . . . "

"Unless they have some kind of magical powers," Liza finished Eddie's sentence.

"Besides," Eddie said, "if they're not elves, what were they doing with all those presents?"

"There are lots of reasons. Maybe they help with Toys for the Needy," Melody said.

Howie pulled his gloves out of his jacket pocket and put them on. "You can't prove that Hollis Bell and his men are elves."

Eddie frowned. "I guess you're right."

"I might know a way. It's what I was thinking about before," Liza said softly. "We can ask the elf expert."

Eddie looked at her and smiled. "Who is an elf expert?"

"Who else?" Liza said. "Santa Claus, of course."

Eddie patted her on the head. "I hate to break it to you, but Santa Claus doesn't hang around Bailey City."

Howie laughed. "He usually only comes once a year, on Christmas Eve."

"Well," Liza said, buttoning her coat,

"there is a department store Santa at Dover's. Maybe he knows something about elves."

"Right, he probably learned all about them in Santa School," Eddie giggled.

Liza put her hands on her hips. "Do you have any better ideas?"

"All right," Eddie admitted. "It's worth a try."

The kids grabbed their book bags and ran down Forest Lane. Around the corner from Burger Doodle Restaurant was Dover's Department Store. A long line was at the entrance. Tiny children, dressed in their best clothes, were jumping up and down in anticipation of seeing Santa. One little boy looked at Eddie and smiled. "I've been a good boy. Santa's going to bring me lots of toys."

Melody giggled. "Eddie hasn't been very good. He'll probably get a bundle of coal."

"Very funny, reindeer face," Eddie grumbled.

Liza looked at the line and sighed. "You two should try to get along. We're going to have to wait for a long time to see Santa."

Liza was right. The kids waited an hour before they got up to Santa. He was sitting on a big red throne with decorated Christmas trees all around him.

"Ho! Ho! Ho!" the department store Santa chuckled. His blue eyes twinkled

underneath his bushy white eyebrows. "These must be some fine students from Bailey Elementary."

Liza and Howie nodded.

"Ho! Ho! Ho!" Santa said again. "I've been meaning to pay Bailey Elementary a visit."

"We'd love to have you," Liza said politely.

"But right now, we have a problem," Eddie blurted.

Santa shifted in his chair and pulled

the kids in close to him. Eddie heard jingling as Santa put his arm around him. "What can I do for you, Eddie?"

"How did he know Eddie's name?" Melody whispered.

"Santa knows everything," Liza whispered back.

Eddie told him about Bell Construction Company and that he thought the workers might be elves. When Eddie was finished, Santa smiled and winked. "HO! HO! Those elves certainly are a hardworking bunch. I've been telling them they need to slow down and let people work out their own problems. But then again, my wife's been telling me that for hundreds of years, too!"

"Problems?" Eddie said. "We don't have any problems at Bailey Elementary. Except that our teacher works us to death."

Santa winked at Eddie. "My elves are everywhere. They can fix anything. But

what they like to fix most are people who can't get along."

Liza shook her head. "They have their work cut out with Eddie. He has trouble getting along with just about everybody."

Eddie sneered at Liza, but Santa just chuckled. "I think there must be more trouble than just one redheaded boy, or my elves wouldn't be there. Keep your eyes open, you'll see."

"See what?" Howie asked.

Santa chuckled again. Then he patted Howie's head. "Elves are magical creatures, my own special helpers. Don't worry about them. When the time is right, they'll disappear."

As Eddie, Melody, Liza, and Howie walked away they heard a jingle as Santa helped a little girl onto his lap. "Ho! Ho! Ho!" Santa bellowed.

"Well, you heard Santa," Liza told them after they were outside Dover's. "We have nothing to worry about."

"Maybe *we* don't," Eddie said. "But those elves do."

"What are you talking about?" Melody asked.

Eddie looked at each of his friends before speaking. "I'm going to prove that Hollis Bell is an elf!"

6

Bailey City War

Eddie marched down the sidewalk away from Dover's Department Store. Liza, Melody, and Howie had to run to catch up.

"Are you crazy?" Liza squeaked. "You can't make Santa's elves mad at you. Then they won't visit Christmas Eve for sure!"

Eddie didn't slow down one bit. "Mr. Jingle Bell is getting on my nerves."

"But what can you do about it?" Melody asked.

"I'm going to have a little talk with him!" Eddie said.

Howie grabbed Eddie's arm. "Your head must be harder than Mr. Bell's hard hat! You can't just walk up to an elf and ask him if he's Santa's helper!"

Eddie jerked his arm away from Howie. "Why not?"

"B . . . b . . . because," Liza stuttered. "That wouldn't be nice!"

Eddie glared at Liza, Melody, and Howie. "Some friends you are! You're always telling me how bad I am. I'm tired of it! I don't have to listen to you or anybody else! Especially a pint-size playground builder!"

Eddie turned and stomped away, leaving his three friends staring after him.

"I've never seen Eddie so mad," Liza said softly.

Melody nodded. "We never meant to hurt his feelings."

"Seems like everybody is fighting lately," Howie said sadly. "Even us!

Liza shivered as a cold wind sent snowflakes swirling through the air. "Maybe we better catch up with him and apologize."

"Good idea, Liza," Howie said. "Let's go!"

Eddie was already at the Bailey Elementary playground by the time his three friends caught up with him. Snow was falling fast and the sidewalks were getting slippery. Several kids were building a snowman where the swing set used to be. But that's not what Melody, Liza, and Howie noticed first.

Gathered on the playground was a mob of parents, and they didn't look happy.

"Who ever heard of letting kids plan a playground?" a man with dark curly hair said. A few parents nodded and mumbled in agreement.

"You can't let kids plan a playground!" Carey's father shouted above everyone's voices. "They won't think about the cost!"

Huey's mother faced him with her hands on her hips. Her face was red, and it wasn't from the cold. "I've had it with

41

you and your talk of money. The ones who use the playground should be the ones to plan it. And that means our kids!"

"She's right," another man with a big bulky coat said. He pushed his way to the center of the crowd and stood right in front of Carey's father. "Besides, your ideas stink."

"How dare you speak to me like that!" Carey's father bellowed.

"Oh yeah?" the other man sputtered.

"Yeah!" And with that, Carey's father reached out and shoved the other man so hard he fell back into the crowd. Huey's mother screamed, and then the whole crowd started yelling and pushing.

"It's a war between the parents of Bailey City," Melody said sadly.

Howie stuffed his hands deep in his pockets. "People shouldn't be fighting at Christmas. This is a time of good cheer and laughter!"

"Not in Bailey City," Liza sniffed. "And even Santa's elves can't make it better."

"What are you talking about?" Melody asked.

"Don't you remember?" Liza asked. "Santa said his elves can fix anything, especially people who can't get along. That's why Hollis Bell and his crew came here. But it looks like it's too late for Bailey City."

Liza looked like she was going to cry, but not Howie. He stuck out his chin and squinted his eyes. "Maybe not," Howie said. "Not if they have help!"

"Who can possibly help Santa's elves?" Melody asked.

"We could!" Howie said triumphantly. "If we were only positive they really *are* elves!"

Melody clapped her mittens together and Liza hopped up and down.

Eddie just smiled. Then he giggled.

Finally he laughed out loud. "I have the perfect idea! Meet me under the oak tree after supper." And then Eddie turned and disappeared behind a clump of decorated evergreen trees.

Dusk came early that evening, along with three inches of snow. But Liza, Howie, and Melody walked through the deepening snow to meet Eddie. The three friends skidded to a stop when they reached the Bailey School playground. Fifteen brand-new evergreen trees were clustered together near the oak tree. Bright lights twinkled from every one.

"We're going to end up with a forest," Melody shivered.

Howie nodded. "Between that new janitor who keeps turning down the heat, and these little short guys planting Christmas trees, it's beginning to look like the North Pole!"

Liza pointed through the trees. "There's Eddie!"

The three friends kicked through the snow to the oak tree. Eddie was waiting for them. He held up an old paper bag. "I have everything we need right here in this bag." Eddie turned the bag upside down. Two dirty sneakers full of rips and holes tumbled to the ground.

Liza, Melody, and Howie stared at the smelly shoes. "What could you possibly plan to do with those?" Melody gasped.

Eddie rolled his eyes. "Don't you know anything? There's a famous story about elves that helped fix shoes. My grandmother read it to me a long time ago."

"Eddie's right," Liza said. "I remember that story. Every night, after the shoemaker went to sleep, elves sneaked into his house and made beautiful shoes."

"All we have to do," Eddie continued, "is leave these old shoes by Mr. Bell's trailer. If Mr. Bell is really an elf, he won't be able to resist fixing these."

"What if we come back tomorrow morning and find the same soggy sneakers?" Melody asked.

"Then we'll know," Eddie told his friends, "that Hollis Bell is nothing but a ding-a-ling!"

7

Twinkling Lights

The next morning snow covered everything, even the two new evergreen trees that had just been planted beside the school. Eddie trudged through the snow to meet Melody, Liza, and Howie under the oak tree. The four kids were bundled against the cold with coats, scarves, and hats.

"Have you checked the shoes yet?" Eddie asked.

Melody shook her head. "We were waiting for you."

"Let's go." Eddie jogged to the construction trailer and quietly sneaked up the steps. Without a word, he grabbed the paper bag he'd left the shoes in, and peeked inside.

"Are they still there?" Howie whispered.

"Are they fixed?" Liza asked.

Eddie held his fingers to his lips and pointed to the oak tree. He walked back to their meeting place without saying a word. His three friends followed.

"Eddie, let me see what's in that bag," Melody insisted.

Eddie held open the bag and the four kids peered inside.

"Nothing," Melody said.

"They're gone." Eddie said.

"No, they're not," Liza whispered and pointed over to the construction trailer. Hollis Bell was jogging up the steps. He was wearing his hard hat, but instead of boots he was wearing a pair of bright white tennis shoes. Tiny lights twinkled on the heels of the shoes.

"He's wearing my shoes!" Eddie squealed.

"Those aren't even the same shoes," Howie told Eddie.

Eddie nodded slowly. "They're mine, all right. They have an orange stripe just like mine used to before they got so dirty."

"Wow! When those elves fix something, they really *fix* something," Liza said.

Howie pointed towards the trailer. "I bet Mr. Bell bought himself a new pair of shoes. They just happen to look like your old shoes."

Melody ignored Howie and giggled. "I have a holey pair of shoes at home. Maybe I'll bring those to get fixed."

"This is great," Liza giggled. "I could get all my broken dolls repaired."

Eddie rolled his eyes. "There is no time to think about dolls and shoes. We have to figure out what we're going to do about Hollis Bell."

"Why do we have to do anything?" Melody asked. "Even if he is an elf . . . "

"He is," Liza told her.

"Even if he is," Melody continued, "what difference does it make? He isn't actually hurting anything."

Eddie kicked at the snow under the oak tree. "Excuse me for being normal, but I get a funny feeling when little men wearing green hats run around making magic."

Howie held up his hand. "Magic midgets from the North Pole may be the least of our worries." He pointed to the blank spot on the playground where the swing set used to stand. "I heard my mom talking on the phone last night. The deadline for the playground plan is today. If no one can agree, we may not have any playground at all!"

8

Strong Magic

Liza stomped her foot and her boot sank into the snow. "What's wrong with everybody? Why can't anyone agree on the playground?"

Howie groaned. "Everybody thinks their ideas are the best."

"Mine is the best," Melody said. "But I could compromise."

"That's the spirit," Liza said. "If only the parents could do the same."

"Carey's dad is on the playground committee and he never agrees with anyone," Eddie said.

"We're sunk," Howie agreed.

"Maybe not," Liza told them. "Remember what Santa said about the elves? They help fix things, including people who can't get along."

"Those elves are going to need awful strong magic if they're going to fix this mess," Eddie muttered, rubbing his hands together to keep them warm.

Melody's eyes got big. "I don't think those elves are going to be fixing anything at Bailey Elementary. Look!"

The three kids looked where Melody pointed. The short men dressed in old work boots and green hard hats poured out of the trailer and climbed into the large trucks. One by one the trucks pulled away from Bailey Elementary and onto the street. Mr. Bell stuck his head out a window and waved to the kids. Then the trucks turned the corner and disappeared down Forest Lane.

"Where are they going?" Liza gasped. "What about our new playground?"

"It looks like we're not getting one after all," a voice said from behind the kids. It was Howie's mom.

"What's going on?" Howie asked.

Howie's mom reached out and rubbed the top of Howie's head. "I'm sorry, but Bell Construction Company couldn't wait for us any longer. They had to leave for another job up north."

Liza looked as if she was going to cry. "It's not fair," she said. "We can't help it if the parents won't agree on a plan."

Howie's mom sighed. "That's true, but it's too late to do anything about it now."

"Don't worry, Liza," Melody said, patting her friend's arm. "We'll get a new playground next year."

Eddie reached down and picked up a handful of snow. He packed it into a tight ball and threw it high in the air. It landed right where the old swing set used to be. "I don't want to wait until next year. The playground is the most important part of Bailey Elementary School, so we need to do something right now!"

Howie's mom smiled. "Good luck, Eddie. I hope you have better luck fixing up the playground than we did."

"Humph," Melody said after Howie's mom left. "Those elves didn't fix anything. Not the playground or the people."

"They definitely weren't elves," Howie muttered. "If they were, we'd have a new playground now."

"We don't even have the old swing set," Melody moaned.

"At this rate, we'll be in college by the time Bailey Elementary gets a new playground," Liza whined.

"Not if I have anything to do with it," Eddie told them.

"What can you do?" Melody asked as the bell rang to start school.

"Just tell everyone to meet at our table at lunch," Eddie told them. "You'll find out!"

9

A Very Special Magic

No playground! By lunchtime the bad news was all everyone was talking about. Even a group of parents had gathered in the cafeteria to talk about it.

"Principal Davis should have let me hire the construction crew," Carey's dad said loudly. "I would have hired a more reliable company."

"It's not Hollis Bell's fault," Howie's mom argued. "We're the ones that couldn't agree on a plan."

"I saw a picture of a playground once," Eddie said just loud enough for everyone to hear. "The people in the neighborhood built it out of wood. There was a castle with a bridge and a dragon-shaped slide!"

Carey's father shook his head. "It's a

nice dream, Eddie. But a playground like that would cost a fortune!"

"Not if everyone chipped in," Liza said before Carey's father could say anything else. "And everybody worked together."

"The kid has a point," a tall man wearing a baseball cap said.

"Aw, it would never work," the lady with hair curlers argued. "No one would agree on it."

"She's right," someone else hollered. "We may as well give up."

The parents and a group of students murmured as they wandered away, leaving the four kids standing alone.

Eddie took a deep breath. "I'm not giving up."

"But what can we do that our parents can't?" Melody asked.

"Plenty," Eddie told her. "All we need is some wood, a hammer, and a sack of nails."

"We don't know the first thing about building a playground," Howie argued.

"And we'll never learn if we don't try!" Eddie told him.

Melody and Howie laughed. "You can't be serious," Howie said.

But Liza wasn't laughing. "Eddie's right. Hollis Bell told us we have a special magic all our own. I think he meant we can fix this mess, if we try."

"You mean you agree with Eddie?" Melody said. "You've never hammered a nail in your life!"

Liza shrugged. "Then it's time I learned!"

"That's the spirit!" Eddie slapped Liza on the back so hard she almost fell down. "Now all we need is a plan!"

Eddie started drawing on the back of his math homework. First, he drew a castle with tall spires and a swinging bridge. "All this could be made from planks of wood," he explained. "Old tires would be the moat."

"Why would we want old tires?" Melody asked.

Eddie grinned. "They're fun to run through!" Then he drew a big dragon. "The slide is its tail," he explained.

"I must admit, that is an interesting design!"

Eddie nearly toppled over when he heard the deep voice. The four kids looked up to see Carey's father towering over them. They had been so busy studying Eddie's design they had not heard him walk up to look over their shoulders.

Eddie stood up and looked Carey's father straight in the eyes. "It's a great plan, and we're going to build it!"

The tall man laughed a deep rumbling laugh. It was so loud, a group of parents huddled by the doors of the cafeteria came to see what was so funny.

"These kids think they can build a playground," Carey's father said with a smile.

The tall man with a baseball cap squinted at Eddie's design, stooping down to get a closer look. "You know, it could work. We could build it right next to that old oak tree."

The lady with curlers in her hair nodded. "My brother owns Bailey Lumber Company. I bet he'd give us a good deal on all the wood."

"I'll donate the nails and hammers," the owner of the hardware store volunteered.

And then all the parents started talking at once. Before Eddie, Howie, Melody, and Liza could count to ten, the parents started bickering about who would be the director of the playground building committee.

"I have the most experience," the tall man with the baseball cap said.

"But I'm the bank president," Carey's father argued. "I can get a loan."

The lady with curlers shook her head. "I'm getting the lumber so I should be the director!"

"Please stop!" Liza squealed. Then she put her hands on her hips and stared until everyone stopped arguing. Liza sighed. "Whenever we do a project in our classroom we work together as partners. That's the best way to get things done, and it's the only way to finish this playground."

"Liza's right," Howie's mom said.

"But every project needs a leader," Carey's dad said.

"Of course," Liza said quickly, before the parents started arguing again. "And it should be someone who knows what they're talking about."

Carey's father stood up tall. "The kid has good business sense!"

Liza nodded. "There is only one person here who knows about this playground. That person is Eddie!"

"Eddie?" the parents gasped.

"Me?" Eddie squeaked.

"Eddie," Liza said. "It was all his idea. He planned it and he convinced you to build it!"

Howie's mom smiled, the lady in the hair curlers chuckled, and the man in the baseball cap laughed out loud.

"Liza's right," Melody told them. "Eddie knows how to get things done."

"She is, indeed," Carey's father said. "Let's hear it for Eddie, the new director of the playground committee!"

Eddie stood up straight and smiled as the small group clapped and hooted. He waited until they stopped, looking everyone in the eyes before speaking. "As the new playground director," he said in his most grown-up voice, "I expect to see everyone on the playground the first thing tomorrow morning. We have a lot of work to do!"

10

A Little Help

"I can't believe we did it," Melody said. It was the day before Christmas and the four kids were walking to the new Bailey Elementary School playground. They had spent the last two weeks pounding nails. At first, only a few parents agreed to help, but as they worked, more and more joined in. Today they were going to put the finishing touches on their brand-new playground.

Eddie smiled. "You have me to thank!"

"You and half the parents at Bailey Elementary," Howie said.

"I never would have believed we could get everyone to agree on anything," Melody said.

"Then how do you explain that?" Liza

pointed to the new playground. A group of parents were in a huddle, staring in the same direction.

A huge red ribbon was wrapped around the entire playground castle, and a giant bow was tied around the dragon-slide's neck.

"I've never seen such a huge bow," Melody whispered.

"That's not the only strange thing," Howie said. "The playground's finished, too."

It was true. All the little things that had needed to be done were finished. Even the parents were scratching their heads.

"Someone sneaked out here during the night and finished it all," Carey's father spoke up. "Who was it?"

"It wasn't me."

"Me neither."

"I didn't do it!"

Not a single parent admitted to the finished playground and the giant red bow.

"I wouldn't even know where to find ribbon that size," Howie's mom laughed.

"There's only one place where you could find a red bow like that," Carey's father said. "And that's the North Pole!"

"It's almost like magic," Howie agreed.

"It was magic," Liza agreed. "Elf magic!"

"We didn't finish this playground because of elves," Eddie sputtered. "We did it by ourselves!"

"Maybe," Liza said softly, looking at the giant red bow. "Or maybe we had a little help . . . elf help!"

Debbie Dadey and Marcia Thornton Jones have fun writing stories together. When they both worked at an elementary school in Lexington, Kentucky, Debbie was the school librarian and Marcia was a teacher. During their lunch break in the school cafeteria, they came up with the idea of the Bailey School kids.

Recently Debbie and her family moved to Aurora, Illinois. Marcia and her husband still live in Kentucky where she continues to teach. How do these authors still write together? They talk on the phone and use computers and fax machines!